Disney Girls

Adventure at Walt Disney World®

A Disney Girls Super Special

Gabrielle Charbonnet

Disney PRESS

NEW YORK

Contents

Chapter One

Fun, Fine Fare, and Fantasy

"Okay, we've had the fine fare," said Ariel Ramos. "Dinner was great. When does the fun start?"

I looked at Ariel in surprise for a moment before I realized she was joking. My friends and I laughed.

"I don't know," I said. "What do you have planned?"

"Hey, it's *your* sleepover," Ariel said. She dropped her voice to a whisper. "And so far, so good."

I groaned. "Don't remind me."

Need some background? First, my name is Isabelle Beaumont. I have another name too, my "real" name, but

I'll explain that in a sec. This was a Friday night in March, and I had finally agreed to host another Disney Girls sleepover. (I'm a Disney Girl, and so are all my friends. I'll explain that later, too.)

My mom had made a yummy dinner of vegetable stew with rice, and now my friends and I were downstairs in my family room, getting ready for some Disney Girl-type fun.

"First, let's close all the blinds," I said. "And the curtains across the patio doors."

Not long after I had met my five best friends, I had hosted my very first sleepover. I had wanted it to be dynamite, but instead it was a disaster! My awful next-door neighbor, Kenny McIlhenny, had spied on us. He had even videotaped us singing and dancing! (We got the tape back.) I was so humiliated that I waited almost six months to have another sleepover.

Tonight, after we were sure we had total privacy, I flopped down on the couch. My *best* best friend, Jasmine Prentiss, flopped down next to me.

"One more week," she sighed. "Then we get a whole week off. Yay, spring break!"

"Yep," said Paula Pinto. "I just want to run around outside all day, every day."

"I'm going to pick a new color to paint my room," said Ella O'Connor. "My dad said I could."

"Maybe I can help," said Yukiko Hayashi.

There you have it: all six Disney Girls. If you walked in right now, you might look at us and think how different we all are. I mean, I'm African-American, with short braids, tan skin, and brown eyes. Jasmine is blond, with green eyes and a few freckles. Yukiko is Japanese-American. She has straight, shiny black hair, beautiful almond-shaped eyes, and ivory-colored skin. Her *best* best friend, Ella, is short, with blue eyes and sandy-colored hair. Paula is mostly Native American. She's tall, with dark brown hair, brown eyes, and lighter skin than mine. Ariel is her *best* best friend, and she has long, bright red hair and blue eyes. We sort of look like a rainbow. But we're more alike than we seem.

For one thing, we all go to the same school: Orlando Elementary. (Ella, Yukiko, and Ariel are in Ms. Timmons's third grade class. Paula, Jasmine, and I are in Mr. Murchison's fourth grade class.) And all of us except Jasmine live in a suburb of Orlando, Florida, called Willow Hill. (Jasmine lives in Wildwood Estates, which is a really fancy neighborhood.)

The main thing we have in common is being Disney Girls. If you don't know what a Disney Girl is, I'm not surprised. After all, it *is* a secret.

I was about five when I realized that I was a Disney Girl. I was watching *Beauty and the Beast* with my mom. As I sat there in the dark, shivers went down my spine, and not just because it was an awesome movie. As I watched Belle moving across the screen, singing about her life, it was like watching myself. Not just *like*. It was me, up there on the screen. I actually had to look down to make sure I was still in the theater next to my mom.

After that, every day I realized more and more that I was Belle. I just *am*. We are the same person. I love books, I want to travel, I love French things—my dad is even an inventor! (He works in the research and development department of a big company.) The more I accepted the idea, the more *Belle* I was. (Belle is my "real" name that I told you about earlier.)

Anyway, finding out I was Belle opened my life to magic. I discovered that magic is everywhere, all the time. Now I can't imagine living without it. At the same time, being Belle meant I had this huge secret that I couldn't share. None of my friends at my old school would relate to it. I couldn't tell my parents, even though they're great. Not being able to share this with anyone was really hard.

Then, last September, my parents decided to transfer me to Orlando Elementary. It totally changed my life! Practically the first person I met was Jasmine. She introduced me to her friends: Ariel, Paula, Ella, and Yukiko. I thought they were amazing. Back at my old school, I had never had a real best friend. Almost right away, I thought Jasmine was *it*. The thing was, I had my big secret. I liked Jasmine so much, but how would she feel about my being Belle?

As it turned out, I had nothing to worry about. One day Jasmine let me in on her secret: she's really Princess Jasmine, from *Aladdin*. If you look hard enough, you'll see that beneath her blond hair and green eyes is a dark, exotic princess. That's who Jasmine really is. As for the rest of us, well, Paula is Pocahontas. Always has been. Ella is Cinderella, of course. She even has a stepmother and two stepsisters. (They're not mean, though.) Ariel is . . . I'll give you some hints. Who has long red hair, blue eyes, lots of sisters, and swims better than most fish? Yep. Ariel is the Little Mermaid. That leaves Yukiko. Another hint:

her name means "snow child," in Japanese. She has seven younger siblings, whom she calls the Dwarfs. Right! She's Snow White.

Do you think it's a coincidence that we all ended up in Orlando? I don't. I know that magic brought us together and made us best buds. Now we hang tight all the time. We can be our true selves with each other. We're connected. It seems totally normal.

"Speaking of fun, fine fare, and fantasy," I said, "my ninth birthday is coming up, a week from Saturday."

"Cool!" said Jasmine. "We should do something for it over spring break. Something different." Suddenly Jasmine shivered. "Whoa," she said, laughing. "I just felt a rush of magic."

"Maybe it was the bean dip," suggested Ariel.

"No, I felt it, too," said Ella.

We looked at each other. Now that I focused on it, the air did feel tingly and electric, the way it does when magic is near. What was going on?

Then we heard my mom and dad come downstairs.

"Hi," said my dad. "I'm glad you're all here."

I thought, duh! Of course we're all here! We're having a sleepover!

"Isabelle, you know your birthday is coming up," said Dad. "So your mother and I have an extraspecial birthday surprise for you."

My eyebrows raised. Wow! Magic in action!

Chapter Two

You Won't Believe This

Some of my favorite things:
  1) Birthdays
  2) Surprises

"An extraspecial surprise?" I asked eagerly. "What is it?"

"Are you having a baby?" Yukiko asked my mom. (Yukiko's baby sister was born last Halloween. Plus she has six little brothers. I guess she figures family surprise = baby.)

"Oh, good heavens, no," said my mom, looking startled.

"You're building a swimming pool in the backyard," Ariel guessed.

"Nope," said my dad.

"You're getting a new pet," said Paula. (Paula loves animals. *All* animals.)

"No," said Mom.

"Is it a new—" Ella began.

"Will you guys let them speak?" I cried, bouncing on the sofa. "We'll never find out what it is!"

My dad grinned. "Well, as you know, I've been working on a big project at work. We finally wrapped it up, and it was very successful."

"What was it?" asked Ariel.

"It has to do with laser-directed navigational systems," my dad began. "My team and I worked out the differential ratio of low-beam emissions to—"

"Honey." My mom interrupted him just when I thought I was going to start screaming with impatience. I would have to warn Ariel about *never* asking my dad to explain one of his projects. He just might tell you!

"My birthday present?" I prompted him.

"Oh, yes," Dad said. "Well, my company gave me a bonus because of our project's success. And here it is." He pulled out some tickets and fanned them in front of us. "Six weeklong passes to the Disney Institute at the Walt Disney World Resort. You can take classes, visit any of the theme parks, whatever you want. This includes the use of a Grand Vista home at the Institute."

My jaw dropped open. "Wha—wha—" I stammered.

"There are six tickets," my mom explained. "One for you, and one for each of your friends. Your dad and I will go along to chaperon, and so will Mrs. Ramos and Mrs. Prentiss. They've already agreed."

My brain shot into overdrive. I could hardly process what was happening. "Did you say—you mean, we're all going to Walt Disney World?" I squeaked. "Together? For a week?"

Mom smiled. "Yep. Here are some Institute brochures. I'm sure you'll each be able to find a class that interests you."

As Mom passed out leaflets, I realized none of my friends had said a word. Looking up, I saw that they were as totally stunned as I was. Ella's eyes were big and round, Paula was grinning, Ariel was practically quivering with excitement. All of a sudden, the reality sank in. One second later, we started shrieking, hugging each other, hugging my parents, hugging my dogs, and jumping on furniture.

"I don't believe it!" I cried, spinning in a circle with Jasmine. "All of us together for a week, at Walt Disney World! It's magic!"

"It *is* magic!" Yukiko agreed breathlessly. "It's a dream come true!"

My parents looked happy that we were all so excited. One by one we hugged them and thanked them.

"I'm glad you approve," said Mom. "Now, we'll leave you guys to plan how you're going to spend your week there. Just try to keep it down to a dull roar, okay?"

"Okay, Mom," I said. "And thank you both so, so much!"

After we heard the door close behind them, the six of us stared at each other.

"Oh, my gosh," said Ariel, holding her hand against her cheek. "I've never even stayed overnight there."

"Me neither," said Yukiko.

"I've only stayed overnight once, when my cousins were in town," said Ella. "Never for a whole week."

"The Institute has some majorly cool classes," said Paula. "I've been dying to take their rock-climbing course."

"I can't believe my mom agreed to be a chaperon," Jasmine said. She opened her brochure and began reading. "Oh my gosh, they have dance classes!" (Jasmine and Yukiko already take ballet.)

I opened my brochure, too. "It'll be like one huge DG sleepover, all week long."

"This is definitely a magic wish come true," said Paula. "We can take our classes in the morning, and do other fun stuff every afternoon."

The brochures were filled with pictures and descriptions of a hundred different choices. I didn't know how I would ever decide. I still just couldn't believe this was happening. If I had wished for a million years, I couldn't have come up with such an incredibly fabulous birthday wish. The best thing of all was that I would be sharing this magical fantasy with my five best friends. Sighing happily, I fell back against my sleeping bag. How would I ever stand waiting a whole week?

Chapter Three

The Magic Begins

Sluuurrrp. I sucked up the last bit of chocolate milk in the carton and pushed my school lunch tray away. When I looked up, Isabelle was laughing at me.

"What?" I said, flipping back my long red hair.

"Are you going to do that at Walt Disney World?" she asked.

I giggled, embarrassed. "I'll try not to slurp," I promised. "Now. Has everyone decided what she's taking at the Institute?"

"The Institute." It sounded so, so cool. Since I live in

Orlando, of course I've been to Walt Disney World like a gazillion times. But I had never stayed overnight. And I had never been to the Disney Institute. This morning, getting dressed for the last Monday at school before spring break, I had batted my eyes at the mirror. "No, I can't make swim practice," I told myself casually. "I'll be at the Institute all week." I pivoted and looked over my shoulder, trying to look cool. "Oh, sorry, Camille," I said, pretending my oldest sister was in the room. "Help you wash the car? No can do. You know, I'll be at the Institute all week." I had been having so much fun that I almost missed the school bus.

Now I was sitting with my five best friends at our usual lunch table in the cafeteria at OE. (BTW, OE stands for Orlando Elementary. BTW stands for By The Way. DG stands for Disney Girls. AER means . . . me! Those are my initials. For Ariel Elena Ramos.)

"Yep," Paula said briskly. She unwrapped the second half of her falafel-pita sandwich. (Paula's family is totally vegetarian. Once I asked her why, and she said, "I don't like to eat my friends." I mean, I really love animals, too, but there is no way I'm *not* going to put pepperoni on my pizza.)

"I've already filled out my registration card," Paula continued. "There's a Level-One rock-climbing course. It's going to be awesome." She took a bite of pita and chomped strongly. I could tell she was already imagining tackling the rock wall.

"How about you, Isabelle?" I asked.

"Storytelling," she said. "Of course."

I nodded. That made sense. She reads more than anyone I know. Once I asked her to go to the mall with me, and she said she just had to finish up an exciting chapter in her book. I almost fell over.

"Well, I've finally decided on karate," said Jasmine. "It sounds so cool, and I've always wanted to try it. Mother is horrified." She grinned.

"Wow," I said. "Cool."

"I'm going for the baking class," said Ella. "I liked messing around in the kitchen when I was making my gingerbread castle. I want to learn how to do it right."

I kept waiting for someone to ask me what I wanted to take. I had pored over the brochure for hours, deciding on one thing and then finding something better. I had finally found the absolutely most perfect class for me. I couldn't wait to tell my friends.

"There's an herbal gardening class," said Yukiko. She began to peel her orange. "It should be pretty neat."

"Well, guess what I want to take," I said eagerly. Five pairs of DG eyes looked up at me. I savored the moment. I knew they would never guess in a million years.

"Acting?" said Ella.

My mouth opened in surprise.

"It's got to be acting," Paula confirmed.

"As soon as I saw the acting class, I thought of you," said Jasmine, nodding.

I folded my arms over my chest. My friends smiled at me.

"Fine," I said. "Suck the fun out of my surprise."

"Okay," said Isabelle, tapping her thermos with a spoon. "We should send our registration cards off today, to make sure they get them in time. Why don't you all give them to me, and I'll mail them this afternoon."

We passed our white cards to Isabelle. I felt like my thunder had been stolen. My friends were getting harder and harder to surprise. I would have to work on it.

After school, all of us except Jasmine got in line for the school bus. Since Jasmine lives over in Wildwood Estates, her mom comes to pick her up. The Prentisses have an ultracool car: a Jaguar. I love riding in it.

Just as the bus was pulling in, Mrs. Beaumont drove up in her Volkswagen Beetle. It's a cute car, too. It's bright yellow, and it looks like a great big M&M rolling down the street.

"Belle, your mom's here," I said.

Isabelle frowned as her mom rolled down the window.

"Honey, did you forget your dentist appointment?" said Mrs. Beaumont.

Isabelle slapped her forehead. "Oops!" She ran to get into her mom's car, then stopped and raced back to us. "Here!" she said, pushing our registration cards into my hands. "I won't be able to do it today. Be sure to mail them, okay?"

"Sure," I said. "No prob."

Remembering to mail cards isn't that difficult, right? Well, it is if you have a million thoughts swirling around in your head like seaweed in a tidal pool. Of course I totally forgot about them. I only remembered because my mom asked me to put a letter in our mailbox right before dinner.

"The mail carrier hasn't come yet," she said, "so this can still be picked up."

That's when *I* slapped my forehead. "The cards!"

I raced to my backpack and pulled them out. I glommed stamps on them, then realized that we had all checked off our classes, but had forgotten to fill in our names and addresses on the other side. "Dang, dang, dang," I muttered, grabbing a pen.

Thank goodness I knew all my friends' addresses by heart. I wrote as fast as I could, then pounded out to the mailbox right as our mail carrier was coming up.

"Here!" I panted, waving the cards and my mom's letter. "Here!"

She took them and tucked them into her mail bag. I collapsed on our front steps. That had been close. But I hadn't let Isabelle down. "Way to go, Ariel," I whispered, pleased with myself.

Chapter Four

What a Grand Vista!

Snap. The first picture I took was of the huge water tower at the edge of Walt Disney World. You know, the one wearing giant Mickey Mouse ears? I felt my skin start to tingle, as if magic was swirling around our car.

Mother glanced over at me and smiled. "Darling, haven't you seen that quite a few times before?"

"Uh-huh," I said. "But this trip is special. I want to remember every second of it. I'm going to start a whole new scrapbook just for this week."

It was a good thing I was belted into my seat in my

mom's car, because I was so excited I felt like I might float out of the window at any second. Sunday had finally come! And our week at Walt Disney World was about to begin. The last week had taken about five years to pass. And now my mom was driving us to the Disney Institute.

"Thanks for being one of our chaperons," I told her as we followed the signs to the Institute. (Walt Disney World is ginormous. Even after you're on the property, you have to drive about fifteen minutes to get to different places.)

Mother patted my leg. "It will be fun, darling. And since your father had to go to Germany for the week, it was perfect timing."

I looked out the car window. "There's the sign!"

Mother turned left and a minute later she pulled to a stop in front of an archway. We were here! *Hello*, Disney Institute! We walked under the archway to the Welcome Center. This was going to be the best week I'd ever had!

Eagerly I pushed open the white door and rushed inside.

"Jasmine!"

Isabelle was running toward me. I lifted my camera and snapped a picture of her. Then we hugged and spun in a circle.

"We got here just a minute ago," Isabelle said, pointing to her parents. "My dad is getting directions to our house."

"I can't believe it," I said. "I still can't believe it!" We were both smiling so big our faces hurt. My mom went over to shake hands with Mr. and Mrs. Beaumont. Then the doors opened again and Ariel ran in, her long red hair streaming out in back of her. Paula was behind her, and Yukiko and Ella came in with Mrs. Ramos.

We all started talking at once, then broke off with a laugh. Mr. Beaumont came over, looking flustered. (He kind of always looks flustered.) He was wearing navy plaid shorts, a white polo shirt, and, get this: dark blue socks with sandals. I bet Isabelle was dying.

When Isabelle saw where I was looking, she rolled her eyes. "What can I say?" she whispered. "He's a brilliant inventor. But a fashion leader, he's not."

I giggled. Mr. Beaumont gave Mrs. Ramos and my mom directions to our Grand Vista home. Then it was back into our cars, and down a bunch of pretty, treelined roads. Mother followed Mr. Beaumont's car and parked next to him in front of a modern wooden house.

I took out my camera and snapped a picture of our home away from home.

"Oh my gosh," said Ariel. "Look! I can see two different pools from this window!" She lowered her voice. "Thanks for letting us all stay in your palace, Princess Jasmine."

I grinned. Inside, our Grand Vista home was, well, really *grand*. There was a big living room, a dining alcove, a full kitchen, two balconies, three bathrooms, and three bedrooms. The six of us raced around, checking everything out.

"This one has a king-sized bed in it!" Ella called.

Isabelle trotted over to her. "This is ours," she said. "Definitely. We can take turns either sleeping in the bed or on the floor in our sleeping bags."

"There's a TV in here!" Ariel squealed. "Our own TV!"

For two hours we ran around, looking in every closet and corner of the house, getting settled. There were little bottles of shampoo and stuff in the bathrooms, all with Mickey Mouse on them. So cool!

My mom and Mrs. Ramos were going to share a

bedroom with two double beds in it. I saw Mrs. Ramos's eyes widen when the porter finished bringing in my mom's luggage. (She had brought three large suitcases for one week. Just for her.) I laughed to myself. My mom and Mrs. Ramos are *way* different. My mom is young and really beautiful and always looks dressed up, with fancy hair and makeup and everything.

Mrs. Ramos is much more laid-back. Like Ariel, she has bright red hair and blue eyes. She likes to laugh and have a good time. Sometimes she can even be as loud as Ariel! In my house, people don't raise their voices. Everything is very quiet and polite. At Ariel's house, when it's dinner-time, Mrs. Ramos stands at the bottom of the stairs and bellows, "Chuck wagon!" It's fun.

The king-sized-bed room had a six-drawer dresser, so we each got a drawer. I was cramming the last of my stuff in mine when Ella flung the door open.

"Come on!" she said. "We're going to head over and check in for our classes so we don't have to do it tomorrow."

"Okay," I said, shoving the drawer shut.

"Then we can hit the restaurant for dinner," said Paula.

"Then we can have an after-dinner swim," said Ariel.

"The Institute has five different pools. We should try each one."

Isabelle nodded. "There's a sand volleyball court I'd like to check out, too."

"And we can watch the fireworks from our balcony," said Yukiko. I hugged myself with happiness. Can you imagine having a better time? I couldn't.

While our parents got ready to go with us back to registration, Isabelle beckoned us over. "Quick!" she whispered. "We're alone for a minute. Secret wish!"

We all linked pinkies and closed our eyes. Usually I have to concentrate for a minute to get in touch with magic, but this time I felt it as soon as I closed my eyes.

We chanted:

"All the magic powers that be,
Hear us now, our special plea.
We trust you to help us pass the test
And make our week here be the best."

Startled, I opened my eyes, and said, "What test? Where did those words come from?"

Ella shrugged. "They just came out of our mouths."

"Maybe it's a test of magic?" asked Paula.

"Hmm," said Isabelle, looking thoughtful. "Maybe it wasn't a coincidence that it's my birthday week and Dad got passes to come here and we're all together. Maybe we're actually here for a reason. A magical reason."

A shiver went down my spine. None of us really believes in coincidences. Usually we can see that whatever's happening is happening for a reason. Was Isabelle right? If she was, what was our magical reason for being here? I would have to pay attention.

Chapter Five

Trust the Magic

We decided to walk to the Welcome Center. There were plenty of paths to follow, and signs showing us which way to go. Ariel and I are used to walking really fast, but we had to keep stopping so everyone else could catch up with us.

I kept my eyes open, searching for landmarks, getting an idea of where we were. Even though there were signs, it's always a good idea to memorize your way back home. I knew I could lead my friends back to the house even in the dark.

"Paula!" Yukiko cried. "Wait up!"

I stopped again. "I can see the Welcome Center through those pine trees," I told her. "It's just a little farther."

Ella's tongue was hanging out. "We should have taken our golf cart," she said. "Or the bicycles."

Yep—our Grand Vista home actually came with its own golf cart *and* enough bicycles for everyone. I was looking forward to trying them, but I was glad to get in some exercise before dinner.

"You're doing great," I told Ella. "We can ride bikes tomorrow."

At the Welcome Center, the parents wanted to try the restaurant reservation computer. The other DGs and I stepped up to the Classes Registration line.

"Hi," said Isabelle. "I'm Isabelle Beaumont. My friends and I have signed up to take classes this week. Can you check to make sure we're all set?"

"Certainly," said the cast member. (All Walt Disney World employees are called cast members. I don't know why.)

She clicked some keys on her computer and looked at her screen. "Yep, you're all set," she said with a smile. "Isabelle Beaumont—your gardening class will be over at the botany center."

Isabelle got a little crease between her brows. "Gardening class?"

"That's right," said the cast member cheerfully. "And the other people in your party—let's see. Ella O'Connor, your acting class will be in the main theater building."

"Acting!" Ella said, looking horrified. "But I wanted—"

"Yukiko Hayashi," the cast member read. "You are in the Level One rock-climbing class."

My eyes opened wide. I knew I was the only one who had signed up for rock climbing. Yukiko looked upset.

"What about me?" I asked. "Paula Pinto."

"You're in Karate 101," she said.

My mouth dropped open. "Karate?"

"And Jasmine Prentiss is in the storytelling seminar, and Ariel Ramos is in the baking class."

Ariel—baking? I thought. Then I remembered Isabelle's mom coming to pick her up at school. Isabelle had handed the registration cards to . . . Ariel.

The other DGs had the same thought. (We do that a lot.)

Five upset faces turned to look accusingly at Ariel. Ariel's blue eyes were wide, and then slowly, a deep red blush crept up her face until she looked like a sunburned lobster.

"Okay, what happened?" I asked her.

Isabelle crossed her arms over her chest. "I don't want to take gardening," she said.

The cast member was looking at us in confusion.

"Um, maybe we should go over here and figure this out," I said, pointing to one of the lobby couches.

Ariel sat down, frowning. "This wasn't my fault," she said. "None of us had remembered to fill in our names and addresses. I had to do it all myself, really fast before the mail carrier came."

"Didn't you read the other side?" Yukiko asked. "There is *no* way I'm taking rock climbing!"

I didn't blame my friends for being upset. I didn't want to take karate at all! I am majorly into nonviolence. Learning how to chop people on the neck sounded awful to me.

"What's the big deal?" Ariel asked defensively. "We'll just ask them to switch us around. Or we'll pretend to be each other. Whatever."

Hmm. I wasn't too sure I could pass for Yukiko Hayashi. Then I had another thought. "Wait!" I said, holding up my hand. "Maybe—maybe we shouldn't switch."

"Of course we should switch!" said Ella. "Like I really want to stand up in front of a bunch of strangers in an *acting* class!"

"I definitely want to switch," said Isabelle. "I've been dying to take that storytelling class."

"Okay," I said. "To tell you the truth, I want to switch, too. I'm totally into rock climbing, and so *not* into karate. But . . . " I paused and looked into my friends' eyes. "What if this is part of the plan? What if this is some kind of challenge for us? I mean, what if magic arranged this for some reason?"

"You mean magic made Ariel goof up?" asked Jasmine.

"I did *not*—" Ariel began.

"Look," I interrupted. "As much as I want to switch back, maybe I should try the karate class. If magic did do this, I want to know why. Maybe karate will help me grow as a person, and as a Disney Girl, somehow." I shrugged my shoulders. Just between you and me, I doubted it.

Ariel narrowed her eyes at me. "And just how is a *baking* class supposed to make me grow as a person?"

"I don't know," I admitted. "But I can't help thinking

that this isn't a *coincidence*. Right? Everything happens for a reason." I sat back and waited as my friends thought about it. Maybe I was making a mistake, trying to talk them into sticking with their new classes. Part of me still wanted to ask the cast member to switch us around. I had even bought new ultralight climbing shoes just for the rock-climbing class. But my DG instincts were telling me to wait a minute and think things through.

"What if it isn't magic?" asked Yukiko. "What if it was just Ariel?"

"I *told* you I—" Ariel said. I could tell she was getting ticked off.

"Then we still get to spend a fantabulous week at our favorite place in the world," I cut in quickly. "We'll have every afternoon to do whatever we want. We'll have a DG sleepover every night. How could that be bad?"

"That's true," said Isabelle thoughtfully. "Well, maybe gardening wouldn't be *too* lame."

"Yeah," Jasmine agreed.

"Well, I'll take baking, I guess," Ariel said. "If I must."

"What about me?" cried Yukiko, holding out her arms. "I'm still stuck with rock climbing!"

"And I have acting!" Ella said.

31

"And I have karate," I pointed out. "But we can't have some of us switching and some not. It's all for one and one for all, right? We all have to agree."

One by one my friends looked at each other, then at me.

"Welllll, okay," said Yukiko, sounding unsure.

"What*ever*," said Ella, not looking at me.

"The rest of us are okay with it," said Jasmine.

"All right," I said. "I guess I am, too." And that was how we decided to put ourselves in magic's hands.

Chapter Six

Dear Diary, Part I

Monday

Dear Vacation Diary,

Isabelle here. Mom and Mrs. Ramos are fixing lunch right now. After lunch, we're going to take a quick swim so we'll be all refreshed for an afternoon at . . . the Magic Kingdom! I can hardly wait.

Before we came here, Jasmine had decided to keep a special scrapbook just for this week. So we're all going to write in this diary, and Jasmine is

taking pictures every five seconds.
(The rest of us are taking pictures,
too.)

This morning we had breakfast here,
because we slept late, because we
stayed up so late last night, and we
didn't want to be late for our—
groan—classes. I had some of Mrs.
Prentiss's smoked salmon on a bagel
with a little cream cheese. Paula had
some muesli with milk. Jasmine had the
smoked salmon, too. Ella decided—
wait. Ariel just read this over my
shoulder and said I was putting in <u>way</u>
too much detail. I guess I should write
about my class this morning. Did it feel
like a magical test? Well, not really. As
you know, I was all hyped about the
storytelling class. But due to circum-
stances <u>beyond my control,</u> I ended up
this morning at the botany center, for
my first herbal gardening class.

Get this. I was the youngest person there. Everyone else (seven other people) was a grown-up. They were all wearing faded khakis and workshirts that looked as if they had seen a lot of gardens. I was wearing black, green, and red leggings, and a short-sleeve red sweatshirt that had a green and black Dalmatian puppy on it. Not to mention the green bandanna keeping my braids out of my face.

(Ariel says I'm still blathering too much. Sorry. All this detail probably would have been fine in the storytelling class.)

Anyway. Our teacher was a nice guy named Dan. We sat on wooden garden benches while he explained a bit about what he does here at the Institute, and his educational background. (Yes. He has a master's degree in <u>gardening</u>. I was, like, okaaaay.) I sat on my bench, swinging my red high-top sneakers back and forth, and wondering what Yukiko was thinking when she signed up for this course. Was Dan going to give us herb recipes or something? Was he going to show us how to make mulch? What fertilizer to use for red, juicy tomatoes? I braced myself to be bored out of my mind. I was glad I was wearing a bandanna because I thought maybe it would keep my head from exploding.

Then Dan started talking about . . . magic. He didn't actually use the word magic, but that's what he meant. He told us about the history of herbs, how they and other plants had been used for thousands of years not only to season food, but as medicines, poisons, and even as part of religious ceremonies. Well! Talk about cool! Did you know that peppermint tea can soothe an upset stomach? Did you know that in the Middle Ages, people thought tomatoes were <u>poisonous</u>, because they're related to the nightshade family of plants? Did you know that some people are totally into <u>parsley</u>, the way cats are into catnip?

Wow! What a revelation! Class was over too soon. I hope it's interesting again tomorrow! —I

Monday

Good grief, I had no idea Isabelle was going to be such a diary hog. I've only been waiting for like practically an hour for her to finish writing her life story. I mean, Geez Louise! We've all got to write in here, snarf down some chow, hit the water, then make tracks for the Magic Kingdom! And there's Belle, going on about, "Oh, I had raspberry jam for breakfast," and blah, blah, blah . . .

Um, Paula just looked over my shoulder and said I was wasting time. Okay. So I should tell you about my baking class. Let me just say this: a magical test, it wasn't. I don't know what Ella was expecting when she signed up for it, but I was thinking maybe we would spend the morning making different kinds of cookies and taste-testing them. Now <u>that</u> I could get into. The only thing that cheered me up was the fact that most of the people in my class seemed even more clueless than I was. One lady couldn't even crack an egg! It got all over her! There was also a boy about my age who looked like he was in major pain being there. I guess his folks made him sign up or something. I'll try to sit next to him tomorrow. We can complain to each other.

Paula just read this and said she thought maybe I was missing the point about writing in this journal, and also missing the point about taking a chance on our different classes. Well, _fine_. I'm going to go take a chance on a hot dog. See ya.—Ariel

Monday

First, let me admit that we are not expected to climb actual rocks. It's actually a man-made rock wall, with built-in handholds and foot notches and things to grab. And before you even get two feet off the ground, they hook you into a harness that someone controls, so it's not like you can fall and go crunch or anything. Those are the good things. The not-so-good things are that the rock wall is still impossible to climb; the fact that everyone gets to watch everyone else, even if they are totally lame and cannot even climb up to like Level One; and the fact that there is a six-year-old girl in my class

who can climb like you wouldn't believe.
She scampered practically halfway up
the wall with no problem. She's human-
fly girl. I wanted to say: I'm Snow
White! Snow White isn't supposed to
climb anything! Help!
   Note to myself: wear leggings
tomorrow. That way my knees won't get
scraped (ouch—total Band-Aid city) and
also I won't have to worry about everyone seeing my Minnie Mouse underwear
peeking out from the bottom of my
short shorts.—Yukiko

Monday
   I just got finished eating, and I've got to
write my part fast while everyone's scrambling
into bathing suits. I can't believe that Ariel
isn't happy about the baking class. It sounds
so cool to me! Which is why I signed up for it.
Anyway. My acting class would be fabulous if I
wanted to act, which I don't, or if I liked
showing off in front of strangers, which I

don't, or if I wanted to develop my natural acting ability, which I don't have any of! Today we started off with actual exercises, like aerobics and stretching, because acting is more than using your face. You have to use your whole body. (Our teacher said that.) Then we went around in a circle and explained why we had signed up for this class, and what we hoped to accomplish. I have to tell you—I lied. Yes. What was I going to say? "I'm in this class because my friend goofed and my other friend convinced me it was a magic test? And what I hope to get out of it is that I don't faint or throw up in front of everyone from nervousness?" I don't <u>think</u> so. I made something up. I don't even remember. My knees were shaking and my voice cracked. Besides all that, it was <u>great</u>. This is going to be a <u>terrific</u> week.

Love, Ella

Monday

Okay, sticking with our new classes was my idea, and maybe I was wrong, but we can't back out now. I mean, I'm the one who really, truly, wouldn't hurt a fly, and here I am in _karate_ class! Hai-yah! Our class took place in what looks like a ballet classroom: there are mirrors covering one wall, and the floor is a special floor that you can fall on and not hurt yourself (at least, not hurt yourself too badly). Our teacher is a guy named (I'm not making this up) Mr. Dasher. Yes, like the reindeer, Dasher is his first name. He seemed nice, but he also seemed like his entire body should be registered as a lethal weapon. First, he explained the rules of the dojo. (He called the room we were in the dojo.) We had to call him _Mister_ Dasher, we had to _bow_ every time we entered or left the dojo, and we had to treat each other with respect. I liked that last rule. Then Mr. Dasher did a little demonstration, showing us some—well, they're kind of like violent dances. He called them _katas_. Every time

42

he did a chop or a kick, he yelled, "Kee-yah!" and I flinched. I felt like I did not belong there at all. Also, out of ten students in my class, I am the only girl. There is a young woman there, and the rest are boys and men. Sigh. I guess tomorrow we start beating each other up. Question: can I be a conscientious objector, in a karate class?—Paula

Monday

Okay, I'm the last one to write, and the others have already raced out the door and leaped into the pool that's outside our house. I'm ready to join them, but I should write this now, while it's all still fresh in my mind.

I wish Belle was taking this storytelling class. I can tell that <u>she</u> would be so into it. I mean, I think it's kind of interesting, but Belle would really <u>love</u> it. This first day our teacher, Marian, started a story with one sentence that she made up, and we went around in a circle, each adding one sentence. So the story could go wherever we wanted it to go. When it was my turn, all I could come up with was: "And then it was dinnertime, so she had to go set the table." So lame! The person after me said, "But as she reached into the silverware drawer, she saw a tiny piece of yellowed paper stuck to the back of the drawer." The next person said, "It was an ancient treasure map!" See? They all seemed to have so much more imagination than I did. But anyway. I'm trying to keep my mind open. And now I _have_ to go jump in that pool!—Jasmine

Chapter Seven

Who Hates Mondays?

I know lots of people hate Mondays because they have to go back to school or work or whatever. But this week, Monday was the best! First there was the gardening class, which had not been bad at all. Then lunch back at the house, a quick swim in water that was the perfect temperature, and now we were at the gates of the Magic Kingdom, with the whole afternoon and night ahead of us.

"Okay," Ella said as our group huddled in front of the gates. "There are four grown-ups and six kids." She pulled out her Magic Kingdom map and opened it. "I think we should split up into three groups, and each take a different route. I've marked these paths in different colors. This way, we'll cover everything, and we can meet at dinnertime at a restaurant right at six o'clock, allowing a half hour for each attraction."

Of course we all started laughing. Ella is the most organized person any of us know. (Okay, so she's a little *too* organized sometimes!) We always tease her about it. Her mom died when Ella was two years old, so for most of her life, she lived with just her dad. Ella ended up running the whole house when she was about five years old. Now she likes to have everything all planned out. I mean, she even maps out a shopping route at the mall, so we don't backtrack and can still hit all our favorite stores! Now Ella has a stepmother (and two stepsisters), so she can be more of a normal kid. But old habits are hard to break, I guess.

Ella blushed when we laughed. "Look, we're going to be here for only a week! And we have a lot of ground to cover."

"I have an idea," Ariel said brightly. "Why don't we just run around and do whatever we feel like? We'll eat when we're hungry, ride rides, stay together, split up, whatever."

Ella looked horrified. "We might miss something! We might do something twice!"

Yukiko put her arm around Ella's shoulders. "It'll be all right," she said soothingly. "This is a *vacation*. We're not going to be graded on this."

"But—" Ella began.

"I have to say, I vote with Ariel," I said gently. "I just want to wander around. I don't want to have to stick to a plan."

"Me, too," said Jasmine.

"I'm with Ariel, too," said Paula. "We should just have a free-form day."

"So!" said my dad, walking up. (He had been parking our car.) "Have you guys decided what you want to do first?"

The six Disney Girls looked at each other. Ella sighed, then grinned.

"Whatever," she said.

"All right!" I said, slapping her a high five. "Main Street, here we come!"

* * *

47

<u>Our Day</u>

Best:

Big Thunder Mountain Railroad—Paula

Space Mountain!—Ariel

I loved Mickey's Toon Town Fair! I want to live there! I mean, if I can't live in my own castle.—Ella

Dinner at the Mexican place in Adventureland. And the Alien Extraterrestrial Encounter—Isabelle

The Skyway to Fantasyland was <u>sooo</u> cool, even if it was a little bit scary. I rode it three times!—Yukiko

The Swiss Family Treehouse was awesome! I wish my house was like that. But my mom would probably decorate it and put little throw pillows everywhere and, like, wallpaper the tree trunk.—Jasmine

Worst:

Chickening out of the line at space Mountain.—Ella

That second ice-cream cone was definitely a mistake. Ugh.—Ariel

Not having enough time to ride the Big Thunder Mountain Railroad twice.—Paula

They made me go into the Haunted Mansion! I will never forgive them! I'll have to sleep with a night-light on for the rest of my life!—Yukiko

I spilled chocolate ice cream on my new white cropped sweater and we didn't have time to go all the way back home and change so I had to wear this sweater with a big chocolate splotch on it all day and even worse, the stain was in the shape of a paw print and it looked like I had been attacked by a humongous, chocolate-dipped Great Dane.—Jasmine

I've already spent practically all my money because I keep seeing the absolute cutest things, like my sun hat, and my giraffe bracelet, and my Mickey socks, and a tiny flashlight that looks like me (Belle).—Isabelle (What will tomorrow bring?)

Chapter Eight

Rocky Going

Have you ever tried to climb a rock wall?

Okay. Well, have you ever tried to climb a rock wall at nine in the morning? How about at nine in the morning when you didn't go to sleep until TWO O'CLOCK the night before because you and all your best friends were so excited about having so much fun on your first day of a fabulous vacation? And you stayed up late talking about everything and then you all got hungry so you tiptoed to the kitchen and made microwave popcorn and ate so much that you couldn't fall asleep for an hour anyway? And then you got woken up at the crack of dawn by someone's mother who—you will not believe this—starts her day by doing aerobics as soon as the sun comes up? And she tried to get us to join her! (I was like, no thanks, Mrs. Prentiss.)

In case you have never tried to climb a rock wall under those conditions, I will let you in on a secret: IT IS MAJORLY HARD.

First of all, we dragged ourselves out of our room and shuffled to the dining table, with our eyes like slits. I was a little stiff because I had slept on the floor the night before. (Actually, the floor is better than sleeping in the king-sized bed—Ariel thrashes all night long and Isabelle is a major cover hog. But anyway.)

After breakfast I practically fell back asleep in the shower. Then we hustled off to our classes. I wore leggings and a long T-shirt. (Oh! I forgot to tell you—Mrs. Ramos is taking tap-dancing lessons. Mrs. Prentiss is taking the tennis clinic. Mr. Beaumont has been getting backstage tours at some of the science exhibits at Epcot, and Mrs. Beaumont has been talking to the chefs at some of the different countries at the World Showcase. I was glad that all the grown-ups were finding cool things to do.)

Okay, back to the rocks. Our teacher, Diane, was so

cheerful and peppy for such an early morning. I wonder if I'm too young to start drinking coffee. I should ask Mrs. Beaumont.

I pried my eyes open and tried to pay attention while she showed us some basic climbing moves. Diane is pretty amazing. She's so strong—her arms are like iron, and her stomach is flat as a pancake. You can see her leg muscles bulge when she climbs. I bet Paula will be like that when she grows up.

Next we took turns trying to use some of the techniques Diane had taught us. Human-fly girl (her name is Penny) immediately scampered almost the whole way up the beginner wall. I wanted to check her sneakers to see if she had glue on the bottoms. Everyone in class did better than we had yesterday—even me. I actually got up to Level Two on the beginner's wall, but then I made a fatal mistake: I looked down. I was only about six feet in the air, but it might as well have been a hundred. I froze and couldn't move. Even though I was in a safety harness, and knew I couldn't fall, I still couldn't get the nerve to move my hand to the next hold, or shift my foot to a higher position. After a couple of supremely humiliating minutes, they lowered me back down.

I was so frustrated! I knew Paula would have aced this, and I was mad that I'd had to take this course which I hadn't wanted to take in the first place. I thought about Isabelle and how much she was enjoying *my* gardening class. Then Mrs. Sapolsky made it to the top of the beginner's wall, and everyone cheered. I gritted my teeth. I looked up at the top. It was so far away. I felt afraid to even try to get up there.

At the same time I suddenly realized that if by some miracle I *did* make it to the top of the wall, I would feel like Supergirl. I mean, if I could tell people I had completed a rock-climbing course, that would be so cool! They would know I was so brave. I could be proud about it for the rest of my life.

I decided that tomorrow, I would go higher.

Chapter Nine

Dear Diary, Part II

Tuesday

Dear Vacation Diary,

I'm writing a special entry today, sort of as an apology to the DGs. You won't believe what happened today in storytelling class.

This morning Marian (my teacher) took us on a nature walk. After we left the Disney Institute meeting room, we took a left down a small path. In two minutes, we were surrounded by trees and wildflowers and birds and squirrels. We all sat down in the middle of a stand of pine trees. I thought, even if I don't want to be in this storytelling class, it's still cool to be sitting out here, enjoying nature.

Marian started class by telling us a little bit about the history of oral storytelling, and why it's neat and important. (Oral storytelling is when people just tell stories to other people. Written storytelling is when it's actually written down.)

What can I say? My mind started wandering. My classmates starting taking turns telling stories out loud. I was wondering what we were going to do for lunch, and also whether I could make it back to that cute shop at Downtown Disney, where I wanted to buy this truly awesome bathing suit coverup.

The next thing I knew, Marian was saying, "Jasmine? Jasmine?"

My head popped up. "Huh?" (I am so sophisticated sometimes.)

Marian smiled at me. "Your turn," she said.

"Um," I said lamely. My brain was whirring like a hamster in an exercise wheel. A story? Moi? Everyone in my class was looking at me, waiting. I thought about what I'd felt yesterday—that these people all had more imagination than me. I felt really <u>dumb</u>. (None of this is an excuse, you guys. I'm just trying to tell you where my head was at, so you'll sort of understand how what happened, happened.)

There I was. All eyes on me. I was doing <u>this</u>, instead of having a great time bashing things in karate. Well, what could I do? I took a deep breath and said:

"Once there were, um, six girls. Yes. And they were all best friends. They were best friends, and they had, um, sort of a secret club."

(Oh. My. Gosh. I do not believe you did this.—Ariel)

"And one night," I said, "they got together

and had a sleepover. One girl had just joined the, um, secret club, and this was her first sleepover."

(JASMINE!!!—Isabelle)

"They were all having a great time," I continued. "Part of having a great time was the girls taking turns sort of, um, <u>singing</u>, and I guess they were probably dancing a little, too. They were, you know, sort of dancing around and maybe singing like into their hairbrushes and into one girl's dad's golf clubs or something."

(Jasmine, you are going to die—Ella)

By now everyone in my class was really interested. They were smiling and paying attention.

(I *bet*.—Paula)

You know what? I realized I was getting into it. I liked entertaining them, telling a story. And after all, guys, they thought I was making it all up. There is no way anyone could have known that some of this story may almost have happened.

(Jasmine, everything in this story happened exactly like you're telling it. I can't believe you!—Yukiko)

Anyway. Like I said, I started getting into it. I sort of imitated how some of the girls were singing, and I pretended to dance around a little bit. Then I told the class about how all of a sudden, the girls heard a clunk against one window. And how they looked up, and ran outside, and saw one of the girls' neighbors slithering over a fence with a video camera.

(Ella's right. You are going to pay for this!—Isabelle)

I'm telling you, the class thought I was making the whole thing up! They were laughing, and one of the said, "Oh, heavens, can you imagine if something like that really happened?"

(Amazingly enough, I _can_ imagine something like that really happening!—Paula)

I might as well tell you. I finished the

story. I told them how Kenny—I mean, the boy in the story—blackmailed the girls, and then how one of the girls managed to get the videotape back somehow, and none of her friends ever really found out how, and how the boy is still a pain. There. Now you know. I'm sorry, and I didn't mean to give away any DG secrets, but it all just sort of popped out of my mouth. Then, when the class was laughing and hanging on every word, I just went with it. It was kind of fun. I didn't mention anyone by name, and I never said anything about being a Disney Girl or a Disney Princess, or anything. So I don't think it's really that big a deal.—Jasmine

(Somehow, I don't know how, and someday, I don't know when, I will get you for this.—Ariel)

Chapter Ten

Add Water and Stir

So far, the best thing about the baking class is the cute Mickey Mouse apron we each get to wear. It's not that I don't like food. I do. I *looove* food. And it's not like I don't want to learn how to make stuff. In fact, I already know how to make a lot of different things: cold cereal with milk, almost any kind of sandwich, a hot dog, even macaroni and cheese (the kit that comes in a box is so easy!). But so far our teacher's pep talk about quick-rising yeast breads hadn't exactly hyped me up, you know?

"Today we're going to start with a very quick and easy

basic: biscuits," said my baking teacher, Deborah, on Wednesday morning. "Biscuits are one of the easiest and most versatile breads you can make. You know what they say—if you have bread, you can build a meal around it. Biscuits aren't just for breakfast."

I sat up on my stool in the kitchen lab. (We all sat on high stools in front of workstations, like science class. Today I was sitting next to the unhappy boy, whose name was Patrick. He still looked pretty bummed.)

"Now," Deborah continued, "I'm sure many of you have made biscuits before."

I nodded. I'd made biscuits tons of times.

"Ariel?" Deborah asked. "Can you tell us how you made your biscuits?"

"It was easy," I said, shrugging modestly. "First, you preheat the oven."

Deborah nodded encouragingly.

"Then you take an *ungreased* cookie sheet," I went on. I felt like a real professional, using words like *preheat* and *ungreased*. All eyes were on me, and I sat up taller and flipped my long braids over my shoulder. Heck, I guess eight years old *is* a little young to be able to handle something like biscuits. No wonder they all looked impressed.

"What next?" Deborah asked.

"Then, you take the can from the fridge, peel off the label, saving the baking instructions," I pointed out, "and whack the can against the edge of the counter."

I saw Deborah's eyes widen. She probably couldn't believe that I remembered all the steps so well.

"The can will pop open," I informed the class. "Take the dough out of the can and separate it into eight biscuits, unless you got the big size, and then there will be only five. Put the biscuits on the cookie sheet, about an inch apart. Pop them in the oven and follow the baking instructions on the label you saved."

I sat back and folded my arms triumphantly. "Voilà! Biscuits!"

For several moments Deborah didn't say anything. Then she nodded and gave me a little smile. "Yes, well, thank you, Ariel. That was very—instructive. I think today we're going to make our biscuits from scratch. You'll find that it's almost as quick and easy as buying the premade kind." She turned to her worktable and began assembling ingredients.

I frowned as Deborah wrote a recipe on the blackboard. Premade? My biscuits hadn't been *premade*. I'd cooked them myself, hadn't I? I mean, the dough was totally raw inside the can, right? What was she talking about?

I decided not to worry about it. You say toh-may-toh, I say toh-mah-toh. That kind of thing. Anyway. I got out my measuring cups and my canister of flour. I looked up at my table partner, who was sitting there looking glum.

"Come on, Pat," I said. "Help me measure baking powder."

"No," he grumbled. "I hate this. The only reason I'm here is because the rock-climbing course was full."

I put my hands on my hips and looked at him. What was this whole class about? What was magic trying to show me, and what did Patrick have to do with it? Frankly, I didn't have a clue. Not yet. What I did have was an empty hole in my stomach that was crying out for hot biscuits fresh from the oven.

I jammed a measuring spoon into Patrick's hand. "Look, you're here now. There's no point in being a weenie about it. You might have hated rock climbing. What if you stank at it?" I asked helpfully. "What would you rather be: a fabulous chef or a totally lame rock climber?"

"Um," Patrick said, looking confused. I pushed the can

64

of baking powder at him and read the recipe on the blackboard. "Measure out one-half teaspoon," I told him. "Did you know that a lot of great chefs are men?"

Patrick wordlessly measured the baking powder. I felt pleased with myself. Sometimes people just have to be pointed in the right direction.

Chapter Eleven

Kee-Yah!

"Kee-yah!" I bellowed, snapping my bare foot toward the hanging bag. *Thunk!* The bottom of my foot connected with a sharp, satisfying kick. Mr. Dasher, who was standing behind the heavy bag, holding it steady for me, nodded.

"Good, Paula," he said in his raspy voice. "I could feel the power."

I stepped back, panting, and bowed crisply. Then I went to the back of the line. The person in back of me walked forward and assumed the stance for a standing side kick.

This was my third morning of karate. Let me tell you, I had had some wrong ideas about it. I had thought karate was all about trying to whack people or break boards with your fist, or smash concrete blocks with your forehead. And I guess there are some karate students who try to do those things. But it's not like that's required or anything.

The way Mr. Dasher had been teaching it, karate was more about self-defense. And while I don't ever want to hurt anyone, it doesn't seem like a bad idea for a girl to know how to protect herself. Plus, Mr. Dasher taught us that conflict should be avoided as much as possible. I should use karate only as a last resort. I like that. Not only that, but it just seemed like plain old good exercise. After every class, I was dripping with sweat. All my friends say I'm in terrific shape, but after karate class, my muscles are actually sore! These classes are a huge challenge, and you *know* how much I love a challenge!

Maybe magic knew what it was doing after all.

"I can't believe how much you're enjoying my karate class," Jasmine grumbled. We were standing in front of the gates to Disney's Animal Kingdom. I had been waiting for this moment for practically my whole life. (That's how it seemed.) As soon as Mrs. Prentiss came back from parking her car, we would enter a whole new wonderful world.

"It *is* weird," I admitted. "I thought I would be grossed out by it. But in a strange way, I'm finding that it really suits me. It's graceful and strong, and it has a purpose. I like it a lot."

"Maybe you should continue karate classes when we get back home," Isabelle suggested.

"Yeah. You and Jasmine could take them together," said Ariel.

"Great idea!" Jasmine said, her face lighting up.

I didn't say anything. I wasn't sure if I wanted to go with karate. I wasn't sure if I liked that image of myself—you know, kind of a "girl warrior." But I could decide later.

"Okay, ladies," said Mrs. Prentiss, walking up to us. "Ready?"

"Ready!" we yelled.

"Thanks for coming with us, Mrs. Prentiss," said Isabelle as we pushed our tickets through the entrance gates. "Mom and Dad were glad to head to Epcot by themselves."

"Oh, I'm delighted, darling," said Mrs. Prentiss. "I'm

glad to have a chance to wear this precious new safari out-fit." She smoothed her khaki shirt down and patted the pockets.

Jasmine and I grinned at each other. I can't imagine my mom saying something like that. My mom never wears makeup (my dad hates makeup), and her hair is long and straight, either in a braid or ponytail. She wears the same kind of clothes I do: comfortable, practical stuff with pockets. I'm really proud of my mom—she just passed her veterinarian exams, so she's a real vet now. She became the partner of another vet at an office in Winter Park, which is a town nearby. I want to do the same thing when I grow up.

In the meantime, I like being a kid! Especially since I'm with my five best friends at Disney's Animal Kingdom!

The first thing we saw when we walked through the gates was the Oasis. It was as if we stepped through a magic door into another world. We went from a regular parking lot—to paradise. Everywhere I looked, there was something beautiful or surprising or fun. We saw so many animals! Tiny deer, iguanas, unusual monkeys . . . Best of all were the interactive exhibits, where we could learn about animals by doing neat, hands-on stuff.

"Hey!" said Ariel, reading a plaque. "This little sign here calls *birds* animals."

"Of course they're animals," said Isabelle.

"Aren't they just *birds*?" asked Ella. "Like insects are just insects?"

"Insects are animals, too," I said. I could not believe this. What rock had my friends been hiding under? How could they not know this stuff? Everyone knows this stuff!

"Insects aren't animals," Ariel said, frowning. "They're *insects*. They don't have fur. They lay eggs."

"You're confusing animals with *mammals*," I said, trying not to look shocked. "Mammals have fur, give birth to live babies, and nurse their young. But *animals* in general are anything that isn't a plant." I know what you're thinking: what about platypuses and echidnas? Well, you and I both know that those are mammals that actually lay eggs. But I wasn't about to confuse my friends with that info.

"What about penguins?" Ariel asked accusingly. "They lay eggs."

"Have you, like, *slept* through every earth science class since kindergarten?" I cried. "Penguins are *birds*! Of course they lay eggs!"

"Penguins are birds?" asked Ella. "Aren't they sort of like seals?"

I took a deep breath and counted backward from one hundred, by sevens. Then, very calmly, I said, "Penguins are birds. They have feathers. They lay eggs. They are not mammals."

"But they're fat, and they don't fly," Ella argued. "Whoever heard of a fat, heavy bird?"

At this point two things became clear: 1) Ariel and Ella had come to Disney's Animal Kingdom in the nick of time. Maybe they would actually learn something. Like, what the difference between plants and animals is. 2) I should not continue this conversation. If my friends said one more unbelievable thing, I would just freak out. I had to move on and do something else.

"I think I'm going to find the Conservation Station," I mumbled, heading off. Only about a minute passed before the Disney Girls caught up with me. Isabelle and Jasmine grinned at me, and I had to grin back. Boy! Are the six of us ever different!

As we wandered through Disney's Animal Kingdom, I saw more cool things than I could have imagined. There were so many unusual animals there, and the setting wasn't like a zoo. Every time I met an animal's eyes, a tingle of magic went through me.

"Oh my gosh," I breathed. "Look! There are two baby lions."

"Oh, so cute!" said Isabelle, peering over my shoulder. "I just want to pick one up."

I laughed. "Even a baby lion could do serious damage without meaning to. They don't understand how fragile people are."

"Look—there's a place where we can pet animals," said Jasmine, pointing.

"Awesome!" I said. "Let's go."

Chapter Twelve

Acting Out

My classmate Brad lay on his side, curled up tightly. I narrowed my eyes, watching him. Today in acting class, we were taking turns being inanimate objects. Somehow we had to express what we were without speaking. Patsy had bent herself into an angular shape. It had been easy to see that she was a chair. Albert had shifted from side to side, making a squeaking noise. He had been a door.

Now we were all staring at Brad, wondering what the heck he was doing. He just lay there like a lump. Maybe that was it! He was a lump of clay, or dirt! Or maybe not.

"Are you a rock?" guessed our teacher, Frederick.

Brad didn't move. I wondered if he had fallen asleep.

"Does anyone want to guess?" Frederick asked.

People called things out. "A turnip?" "A hunk of wood?" "A piece of cement?"

Finally Brad uncoiled himself and looked at us with disgust. "I was a *seed*," he said grumpily.

"I was about to guess that," Susan said.

I thought, I'm *so* sure.

"Brad, how were you projecting seed qualities?" Frederick asked.

Brad stood up and threw his arms out to the sides. "I was projecting hope! I was projecting *possibility*!"

"Ah," said Frederick. "Okay, we can work on clarifying those projections."

Like how? I thought. Like with a neon sign?

Even though I thought Brad was being silly, some of the others had been pretty neat. One of the good things about this class was that there weren't some people who looked cool and some people who looked dorky. We *all* looked majorly stupid. It was kind of comforting.

Take yesterday, for example. We had all been different

animals. I had been a mouse. I just thought about how my pet mice, Jacques and Gus, act, and tried to act like them. My classmates had all agreed that I was very convincing as a mouse. That had made me feel good. So the animal exercise had been fun. Today's objects were a lot less interesting.

"Ella?" Frederick said. "It's your turn. Please go onstage. Do you have an object in mind?"

I nodded and began to climb the steps to the small stage at one end of our small theater building. Guess what. After four days of seeing all my classmates doing the most embarrassing things you could imagine, I didn't feel too weird anymore. I blended. It didn't matter if I tripped and fell flat on my face and rolled off into the audience screaming the entire time. Believe it or not, I had seen worse during this past week.

I walked on stage. Frederick clapped his hands for quiet. All eyes were on me. I got on my knees, making sure my feet were straight out in back of me so no one could see them. I stuck my arms tightly to my sides and sucked in my cheeks, trying to look as thin as possible. Then slowly, I started to take my arms out at the sides. Very slowly, I stood up tall on my feet. My cheeks rested normally for a moment; then I puffed them out, just a little at first, then more and more.

By the end of a couple minutes, I was huge and puffy. My eyes were bulging out, my arms were far out and curved, and I was on tiptoe. I felt enormous.

"Class?" Frederick asked.

"A puffer fish?" called Tim.

"A mosquito that just bit someone?" suggested Susan.

Frederick shook his head. "Remember, it has to be an inanimate object. Nothing alive."

"A sponge?" Amber said.

Finally I couldn't hold my breath anymore. It burst out of me and I deflated, sinking down on to my feet and letting my arms drop to my sides.

"Did we guess correctly?" Frederick asked.

I shook my head, trying to catch my breath. "I was a grain of rice, being cooked," I explained.

"Ahhh," said Frederick. He stroked his moustache and nodded. "That was very good, Ella. Even though we didn't guess the exact thing, you'll notice that everyone thought of something inflating, expanding, becoming full. So you projected those qualities beautifully. Also, I'd like to point out that Ella has shown us that an inanimate object does not necessarily mean an object that is completely still. Her grain of rice, while not alive, still managed to inspire or evoke feelings of growth, of change, of a dynamic transformation. That was very well done indeed, Ella. Thank you."

I blushed and trotted off the stage. I was pleased but also a little overwhelmed. Geez, I thought, as I joined my classmates. Frederick sure can wring a lot of meaning out of a grain of rice. Is that what acting is all about?

Chapter Thirteen

Dear Diary, Part III

Thursday

Once upon a time, there was a princess. She was strong and wise and good, but she was very lonely. Her parents, the king and queen, were kind and loving, but they were very busy. Although the princess loved them very much, still, she hoped for someone her age to play with. But her only companion was her imagination.

Then one day, she heard one of the palace guards speaking about a traveling band of enter-tainers who had recently come to town. They had set up their tents right outside the city walls, not far from the marketplace. The princess hid behind a silken velvet curtain and listened to the guard tell his friend what he had seen.

"They have colorful tents!" the guard said in his gruff voice. "They had dancing girls, and brave swordsmen doing tricks! There was a magician who made a length of rope dance. And there was a spinner of tales . . . oh, my friend, a spinner of wondrous tales."

The friend leaned closer. "What manner of tales told he of?"

The guard shifted his spear in his hand. "Not he, my friend, but <u>she</u>."

To be continued . . . by Jasmine Prentiss

Thursday
Continued when? You've got to finish it now! Who is the storyteller? What kind of stories? Are you going to tell us? I'm going to go crazy waiting for you to finish!

Okay, okay. I'll quit griping at

Jasmine. But I guess we can all tell that she's really gotten a lot out of her storytelling class. And thank heaven she's not telling stories starring the Disney Girls anymore!

You know what? I've gotten a lot out of my rock-climbing class. Hard to believe, but true. I'm almost sad that tomorrow is my last class.

Today I used some weight-switching techniques that Diane told us about. Basically, you take turns switching your weight from one foot and hand to the other. This helps you conserve energy and keeps your muscles from freaking out too early. This morning, I found it really helped. Usually my leg muscles start shaking at about the top of the second level. Today I made it all the way to the third level! I looked above me and saw that I had only one more level to go and I would be at the top! I got so excited that my hand slipped and knocked my foot off its perch and I fell off the wall. Of course, my spotter below was holding the rope of my safety harness, so I didn't actually go splat on the ground. I just dangled there, so mad at myself, and then I got lowered slowly to the bottom.

Tomorrow, I promise myself, I will make it to the top. I can do it. There's no point in being afraid. If I concentrate and connect with what I'm doing, magic will flow through me and I will get to the top of the rock wall. I will do it! I will pass magic's test!—Yukiko

Thursday

I'm glad Yukiko is enjoying my rock-climbing class. I will definitely be back to do it myself someday. In the meantime, I have to say, karate is turning out to be pretty cool. I think I might just start

taking classes when I get home. I mean,
karate isn't just for tough guys. It could
really work for anyone. And why shouldn't
girls know how to defend themselves?
Frankly, I think every girl would enjoy that
surge of power you get when you do a spinning roundhouse kick right into a heavy bag.
Of course, now I have blisters on the
sides of my feet. And my knuckles feel a
little bruised from doing knuckle push-ups.
But I love the sense of discipline that Mr.
Dasher, our sensei, gives us. (Sensei
means teacher. We have to use all the right
terms.) And the katas are so cool—they're
a lot like choreographed dances, except
they use moves that are used in karate. I
don't know—it's just really awesome! I feel
like Wonder Woman!—Paula

Thursday
   Okay, there's a little corner of our
yard that gets sun all the time, and

no one's using for anything. So that's where I'm going to put my own herb garden. I've already asked Mom about it, and we're planning it together. She said if I grow enough herbs, I could even harvest them and sell them at Beaumont's! That would be so cool!

I'm going to start with two different kinds of basil (green and purple), two different kinds of parsley (curly-leafed and Italian flat-leafed), rosemary, tarragon, oregano, thyme, spearmint, and peppermint (did you know those flavors came from plants?), not to mention the chamomile, feverfew, slippery elm, burdock root, and some other herbs that can be used to make teas when you don't feel well. I can tell I'm going to be doing a lot of reading about this!

And you know, a lot of my favorite fantasy books have mentioned herbs and plant medicines and stuff, and now I know so much more about it. It's weird how if you learn about one thing you find like five other things that are all related to it. Is everything like that?—Belle

Thursday

Get this: I made chocolate-chip cookies today all by myself, and they were <u>fabulous</u>! I'm not talking about slice-and-bake, either! I made them from scratch, using real flour and separate chocolate chips and everything! And it wasn't that hard. You know, if I really pay attention and follow the directions and do things in order, it usually comes out okay. Why hasn't anyone told me this before?

Oh, I have to tell you—my mom is so into her tap-dancing class.

(Ariel—we've noticed.—P)

It's like she's living out her childhood fantasy or something. It's so funny. Today we were walking through Frontierland and Mom suddenly just had to show us a little tap-dancing routine right there on the wooden sidewalk. She said she loved the sound of her heels on the wood. The DGs and I just looked at each other and laughed, and we all clapped when she was done. A bunch of people had stopped to watch her, and they clapped, too. Mrs. Prentiss looked a little embarrassed. I think she's not used to being the center of attention, like, in front of a bunch of strangers. But my mom sort of lets it all hang out. I was proud of her.—Ariel

Thursday

I already told you all about acting class, and about how my cooking grain of rice was a big hit. Now I'll tell you about Space Mountain. Okay, so Yukiko and I had promised each other we were going to ride Space Mountain sometime this week. There were only a few small obstacles: 1) We're both a little nervous about roller coasters. 2) I don't like being in the dark, and Space Mountain is all in the dark. 3) Yukiko is afraid of going very fast, and it is, after all, a roller coaster.

But this trip we are determined to conquer all those things. We're just having a little trouble doing it, that's all. I mean, was it our fault that it was lunchtime and we couldn't wait in the line any longer? Okay, okay, so it was our fault when we suddenly yelled, "No! We can't do it!" at the last minute and broke out of the line and ran all the way down. But that was just a mistake. We didn't mean to do that. Look at the bright side: today we made it to the very front of the line. We were <u>just</u> about to get on (we really were), but then Yukiko realized she had forgotten to go to the bathroom. So what could I do? We had promised to do it together. I couldn't let her not go by herself. So I didn't go, too. That's what best friends are for. We still have all of tomorrow and all of Saturday. We <u>will</u> do this. We will.—Ella

Chapter Fourteen

Dear Diary, Part IV

Friday

Today I was so sad saying good-bye to my teacher Dan. He gave each of us a small potted rosemary plant to take home with us. And we each got a gardening certificate showing we completed the course. I'm going to take my rosemary home and plant it right away in my corner garden. (After I mix some humus into the soil, and maybe some peat moss so air can get in, and then I have to check the pH balance of that area and fix it if it's too acidic or too alkaline.)

Anyway. In one of my favorite books, <u>Once More the King</u>, the wizard Bantock gives a whole warning about how powerful plants are for good and bad. Now I know what he was talking about. And I feel a little bit like a wizard myself. A plant wizard.

—Isabelle

Friday

Then maybe I'm an acting wizard! No, seriously, guys, I'm pretty sure I won't want to take any more acting classes. But I'm not sorry I took this one. It just goes to show you—sometimes things you hate are just things you don't know about yet. I ended up learning a lot about acting. And about myself. Like, I'm still totally shy in new situations. It's just how I am. But I think I could use acting techniques to feel more confident in front of strangers. And I could use some acting techniques for when I have to give oral reports at school. stuff like that. so I have to say, I'm glad I ended up in that acting class—even though at first I thought it was awful. Thanks, Ariel.—Ella

Friday
  Well, you guys will be impressed. I made it to the top of the rock-climbing wall.
  (Whoa! High five!—Isabelle)
  (Me, too! I am so awed—Ella)
  I just—did it. I made up my mind, I listened to all of Diane's instructions, and right before I started, I closed my eyes and asked magic to help.
  (What, like, "Magic, push up on my butt"? —Ariel)
  Hardy har-har, Ariel. But no. Not like

that. I just remembered when I was back in the forest, running away from the hunter. I was terrified by everything. The black trees, the shadows, the sounds of the forest, the glowing red eyes I saw peering at me—I was <u>so</u> freaking out. Then, when I stopped and calmed down, it turned out I had been afraid for nothing. The animals and trees were fine—they were my friends. I was safe in the forest, protected. Well, that's how it was on the rock climb. I had to let go of my fear, and trust in magic to help me.

(Cool. —Paula)

So I made it. I did it. And I feel really proud, and stronger than ever. And, if I can do that, Space Mountain is going to be a cinch!—Yukiko

Friday
Good for you! We're all so proud of you! Today was my last karate class. I asked

Mr. Dasher if he knew of any karate dojos in Willow Hill. And guess what? He actually is about to open his own dojo (with two other teachers) about six blocks away from Willow Green! I could ride my bike there. So I'm going to sign up. Jasmine, want to do it with me?

(Yes!—Jasmine)

This whole week has been such an eye-opening experience. I feel like I've been reminded to look at things in a bunch of different ways—and to give new things a chance. And of course, I've had a blast with my five best friends. You guys are fab.—Paula

Friday

Guys, the sound you hear is the sound of me puffing up with pride. And I deserve it! Our final test today was the meringue on top of a lemon meringue pie. At first something weird happened with the egg whites I was beating. They just didn't work. But I tried again, and I got it! My meringue was perfect! It looked just the way it was supposed to, and it was totally munchable. Not only that, but I really think I helped Patrick come out of his shell. He actually asked my advice on the best way to cream together butter and sugar. Did you know that when you cream butter and sugar together, no cream is actually used in the process? Cooking is full of weird stuff like that! I feel like I've been let in on a whole bunch of cool secrets.

(Does this means you're going to provide slightly better snacks at your sleepovers? —Paula)

Hey, sleepovers demand Chee-tos! Everyone knows that. Now, enough of all this writing. I'm ready to hit Blizzard Beach!—Ariel

Chapter Fifteen

Bonjour!

We had already had a Jasmine afternoon in Morocco, so I was happy to go with Isabelle to France on Friday. I have to say, Mother and Mrs. Beaumont were so cool. They stayed close enough to keep an eye on us, but we still had total privacy and could talk and be ourselves.

Soon Mrs. Beaumont called Mother over to a small wheeled cart where a cast member was hosting a caviar tasting. Isabelle and I both decided to pass. I've tried caviar a bunch of times, and it doesn't really blow my hair back, you know?

"Oh, look," said Isabelle, pointing. "A sidewalk artist. Let's have her do our portrait. I have some money left."

"Me, too," I said. "We'll split it."

It was really fun having our picture done. The artist worked in pencil and charcoal. Isabelle and I sat right next to each other, our faces turned to the artist. She worked quickly, and didn't speak to us much. We tried to keep very still. After a while I got a crick in my neck, and my face hurt from smiling for so long.

"Just a few more minutes, girls," the artist murmured, sketching intently.

At last the artist sat back and cocked her head, looking at her drawing. "There!" she said, sounding pleased. "It's finished."

We leaped up and ran around her easel to look. When I saw the finished sketch, I almost gasped. Isabelle and I stared at the drawing, then at each other, then at the drawing.

Mrs. Beaumont and my mom came up behind us. "Oh, you had your portraits done! What a good idea," said Mrs. Beaumont. Then she frowned. "It's very nice—but . . . I don't think it really looks much like you two, does it?"

The artist raised her brows in surprise, and looked from us to the drawing. "Really?" she said, sounding confused.

I didn't blame her—or Isabelle's mom. See, the drawing *did* look exactly like us—as Belle and Princess Jasmine. So it didn't look all that much like our everyday selves. Isabelle's skin was too light, and the artist had drawn her little braids as being more pulled back flat against her head. And she looked older. My portrait made my blond hair seem much darker than it is, and longer. My green eyes looked very dark and deep. There were no freckles on my nose. Our picture looked almost exactly like how we *feel* inside.

"You don't have to pay, if you're not satisfied," said the artist doubtfully. "I *thought* it was a good likeness . . . "

"We love it," I said firmly. "We'll take it."

"Yes," said Isabelle, digging out her money. "It's perfect."

"Oh, good," said the artist. She wrapped the picture up in brown paper and tied it with string.

"Mother, I want to have this framed," I said as we walked away. "Then Isabelle and I can take turns hanging it in our rooms."

"It was kind of you to not want to hurt the artist's

feelings," said Mrs. Beaumont. "But really, it doesn't look a thing like either of you."

"I agree," said my mom. "My goodness, she made you a brunette!"

Isabelle and I smiled secretly at each other. Obviously, the artist had seen beyond our ordinary selves to our real, magical selves. Probably because we were in a really magical place. For about the twelve millionth time, I felt so happy and special to be a Disney Girl.

"Ooh, there's the pastry shop," Isabelle said.

"Let's go!" I cried. "I want a chocolate éclair."

"A strawberry Napoleon for me," said my mom.

"Count me in," said Mrs. Beaumont. And we plunged into the pastry shop together. It was a perfect day.

Chapter Sixteen

To Space and Back

Guess what? When you have six little brothers and one baby sister, it takes almost a whole week (and all of your money) to buy souvenirs for them. Thank goodness my mom had given me some extra cash to get all the Dwarfs Mickey ears. Otherwise I would have had to advance my allowance till I was about fourteen years old.

"Um, can I get a group discount?" I asked the cast member who was embroidering everyone's names on their ears.

She smiled me at me. "No, I'm sorry," she said. "Are these for all your classmates?"

"Uh-uh. My brothers and sister," I answered. I saw her eyes get bigger with surprise. I guess she hadn't seen too many families with eight children. But my mom had four of us, my stepfather Jim had three of his own, and then last Halloween they had my baby sister together. Now eight kids in the family seems normal to me.

"Are you almost done?" Ella asked, coming up with a big shopping bag. Mr. Beaumont was right next to her. He'd been a great sport all afternoon, but he was starting to look pretty bushed. His dark brown socks were sagging down around his sandals.

"Almost," I told her. "Two more ears to go."

"They're going to love them," Ella said. She fished in her shopping bag and pulled out a sweatshirt. It said "Remember the Magic." "This is for me," she said, grinning.

"That's great. I have to get one, too," I said. The cast member finished Suzie's name, and I paid her.

"Wow, kids, look at the time," said Mr. Beaumont. He held out a watch so complicated that I couldn't even tell where the hands were. He loves little gadgets. "We should probably start heading back to Liberty Square to meet the others for dinner."

"Let me see the best way to get there," Ella said, pulling out her map and her highlighter pen. She'd found a highlighter that she could wear on a string around her neck. It made her so happy. Ella's pretty funny sometimes.

"Hmm," she said, tracing a route. "We're at the opposite end of where we need to go. And we have to carry these heavy bags."

"Nope. We can take the Skyway right to Fantasyland," I told her, pointing to the map. "Look, it lets us off right there, and then Liberty Square is next door."

"Brilliant!" Ella said, folding up the map. "Perfect."

"Sounds good to me," said Mr. Beaumont.

We started schlepping our shopping bags toward the Skyway entrance. Well. Guess what is about fifteen feet away from the Skyway entrance? Yep. The line for Space Mountain. Ella and I saw it at the same time. We looked at each other. Since it was almost dinnertime, the line was practically empty. Tomorrow, all of us were going to spend almost the whole day, our last day, at the Disney-MGM Studios. This was our last chance. It was now or never.

After I had reached the top of the rock wall this morning, I had felt invincible—totally ready to take on Space Mountain. Now, standing at the entrance, suddenly, I wasn't too sure. I thought I could hear people screaming even from way out here.

Then I looked at Ella. All of a sudden, she turned to me with a determined smile. The same kind of smile Ariel gets when there's a sale on at Zap 2000, her favorite store at the mall.

"We have to do it," Ella said.

A tingle of excitement made all the little hairs on my arms stand up. I giggled nervously. "I know."

Mr. Beaumont agreed to wait for us by the exit with our shopping bags. (I think he was glad to sit down for a minute.) Ella and I raced up the ramp. My heart was already pounding. At the top, we saw that it was the least crowded we had ever seen. In fact, we could go on the very next turn. And guess what? The way the line broke up, Ella and I were in the very first seats in the very first car. But before we could leap out and change our minds, a cast member had fastened the safety harness. It was too late.

Ella and I clutched the bar of the safety harness and stared straight ahead. I felt so nervous and scared but also so thrilled that we were finally doing it. It felt great. All we could see was blackness and a few tiny lights that looked like stars. Just knowing that in a few seconds we would shoot forward into that darkness was enough to make my mouth dry and my heart pound so loudly I could actually hear it.

Then Ella's hand reached out and groped for mine. We could just barely reach each other enough to link pinkies. As soon as we did, I felt much better. Then our car jerked forward, and we were on our way.

I won't tell you what it's like inside Space Mountain. If you've already been on it, you know what it's like. If you haven't been on it yet, I don't want to spoil it for you. Anyway. I'll just tell you that it's the most awesome, amazing, funnest, scariest ride ever. (I know Paula and Ariel think a couple of other attractions are the ultimate. But Ella and I weren't ready to even try those. For us, Space Mountain was the peak.)

When our car screeched to a halt, and we slowly pulled forward to the exit area, I was stunned. My knees felt wobbly, and I was panting. The safety harness rose automatically, but Ella and I just sat there for a few moments. I looked over at her, and we realized we were still holding pinkies. We let go. My fingers were cramped from holding on so tightly. Ella's sandy blond hair was all fluffy from being upside-down. Her eyes were wide. She had a weird smile on her face.

"We did it!" she croaked.

The two of us scrambled out of our car. Behind us more people were waiting to get on. Already the line was longer. My watch said that we had only been gone about three minutes, but it felt like days since we'd seen Mr. Beaumont. We walked quickly down the ramp to the exit, and we saw Isabelle's dad, sitting on a nearby bench, reading a science magazine.

The three of us got onto the Skyway headed for Fantasyland. I love the Skyway. It is so cool to look down and see everything, practically the whole park, and all the people walking around. It's like being a bird.

At the other end of the Skyway, we jumped off, struggling with our shopping bags. We took a quick left and were already at Liberty Square.

"Guys! Over here!" called Isabelle, waving us over. "I can't believe you're late! Ella's never late!"

Then her brown eyes locked onto mine. You know the DGs are all connected, right? She put her hand over her mouth. "Oh my gosh," she breathed. "Did you two do it?"

I nodded proudly.

"You rode Space Mountain!" Isabelle said. "Congratulations!" She hugged us both. Ella and I smiled.

"That's terrific, you guys," said Paula. "Now, let's eat." As I sat there in the Liberty Tree Tavern, surrounded by my best friends, I felt so happy that it was only the huge dinner I snarfed down that kept me from floating up into the ceiling. My life felt like total and complete perfection. Thanks, magic.

Chapter Seventeen

Nine Is So Fine

"Boy, I can't wait till I'm nine," I muttered. I put on the oven mitts and pulled the cookie sheet out of the oven. Today was Isabelle's ninth birthday. The five of us DGs and our parents had been plotting and planning all week.

"First, Ariel's famous biscuits," I said. These were biscuits made from *scratch*, not from a can. I must say, they looked pretty dang good. Okay, maybe they were a teensy bit too brown on top, because I had gotten caught up with seeing if I could loop my braids on top of my head and stick them there with barrettes, so I didn't take them out (the biscuits) at *exactly* the right moment, but they would still taste fabulous.

"Here," said Ella, shoving a napkin-lined basket at me. "Dump them in here and put them on this tray. And hurry! She's going to wake up any second!" Suddenly Ella leaned against the wall and put her hand to her head. "Oh, this is déjà vu all over again," she moaned. "I feel like I'm back with my evil stepmother, making breakfast for everyone before they wake up. Not Alana," she added quickly. "The other one."

I nodded and patted her shoulder. "Snap out of it, Cinderella," I said sympathetically. "This is a whole different ball game."

"Right, right," Ella muttered, and grabbed the juice out of the fridge.

This morning the five of us had gotten up early and sneaked out of our bedroom, leaving Isabelle alone in the king-sized bed. Now Mrs. Beaumont was brewing coffee, I had made biscuits (from *scratch*), Ella was organizing the whole thing (like I had to tell you that) and everyone was getting ready to make Isabelle's turning nine absolutely unforgettable.

Nine! It sounded so old. I wouldn't be nine for months. Nine is right next door to ten, and when you're ten, you're practically a teenager. You have two numbers in your age. It seemed like forever till I would be ten.

"Okay, everyone ready?" Ella asked. "Let's go."

We sneaked upstairs. (Five DGs, plus four parents. You do the math.) Paula silently eased the bedroom door open. (She's amazingly good at being silent. I always bump into things, or hum or something, and give myself away.)

In the bedroom, I covered my mouth to smother my snickering. A king-sized bed is so huge, but Isabelle was taking up almost all of it. Her mouth was hanging open, but she wasn't snoring, unfortunately. If she had been, I would have run to get the video camera.

"One, two, three," I whispered. "Go!"

The five of us DGs ran forward and leaped onto the bed all at once. We practically bounced Isabelle right off the mattress!

"What? What?" Isabelle exclaimed sleepily, brushing her hair out of her eyes. "What's wrong? Is there a fire?" She blinked her big brown eyes and looked blearily at us. "What's wrong?"

"Happy Birthday to you," I sang loudly. One by one, everyone joined in. By the time we finished, you could probably hear us singing "Happy Birthday" in Alaska!

Isabelle's confusion changed to sleepy happiness. She leaned back against the pillows, put her hands behind her head, and beamed.

"Thanks, guys," she said when we had finished. "That's a fab way to wake up. Can you do it every morning?"

"Yeah," Jasmine said. "I'll have my mom give me a ride over to your house every day, first thing."

"Voilà!" I said, pointing to the breakfast tray that Mrs. Prentiss was holding. "Check out the biscuits."

"Oh my gosh!" Isabelle said. "This is so beautiful!"

"Mrs. Prentiss set your tray," said my mom, taking a sip of coffee. "With the lace doily and the flower and all. So everyone has made a contribution except me. Now it's my turn."

I felt a little thrill of worry. My mom can be kind of wacky sometimes. She's not exactly like other moms.

She put down her coffee mug and said, "I have to do this in the bathroom because I need a hard floor." She stepped into the doorway of the bathroom, and started doing a "Happy Birthday" tap dance. She had really gotten into her lessons over the past week. Isabelle looked like she was about to laugh, but in a nice way. I was kind of impressed by how much Mom had learned in just five lessons. I started bobbing my head in time to Mom's tapping feet.

Then, we were all shocked by Mrs. Prentiss squeezing by my mom, and joining in! She tap-danced in the bathroom, doing the same routine as Mom! I had *never* seen Mrs. Prentiss do anything like this! Jasmine looked shocked, too. It goes to show you—just when you think you know your parents, they come up with something weird and totally rock your world.

When they were done, we all whooped and clapped. They bowed to us, and then—get this—my mom and Mrs. Prentiss *hugged*.

"That was incredible, Mother!" Jasmine said. "I didn't know you could tap dance!"

Mrs. Prentiss blushed and patted her perfect hair back into place. "Yes, well, tap dancing was an elective at my college."

"This birthday is getting better every minute!" said Isabelle.

"And you haven't even opened your presents yet," said

Mrs. Beaumont. She and Mr. Beaumont handed Isabelle one medium-size box, one small, flat box, and one envelope.

"What's all this?" Isabelle asked, starting to tear open the paper. "Oh! So fab!" She held up a white T-shirt that was embroidered all over with tiny flowers. It was adorable. (To tell you the truth, Isabelle is about the only DG besides me who has any fashion sense at all.) Then Isabelle ripped open the next package. I started to think about what I wanted for *my* ninth birthday.

"The new Honeygirls CD," Isabelle cried happily. She flipped it over and read the contents. "Yes! It has 'Grrrlfriends' on it! All right! Thanks, Mom. Thanks, Dad."

"You've got one left," Mr. Beaumont pointed out.

Isabelle slit the envelope and pulled out a card. "A gift certificate!" she announced, waving it around. "To my favorite bookstore! This is perfect, because one of my favorite authors is starting a new series all about magic and unicorns and castles and stuff. Oh, thank you, thank you, thank you!"

Isabelle jumped up and hugged and kissed her parents. They hugged her back. Then Isabelle turned around and beamed at all of us. "Thanks, you guys."

"Okay, now get your butt in gear," I ordered. "We have a whole day left."

"Yeah—we don't want to waste any time," Jasmine said.

"I'm up, I'm up!" Isabelle yelled, yanking open her dresser drawer and grabbing a pair of jeans. "Let's go!"

Chapter Eighteen

Happy Birthday to Me!

I just loved the Disney-MGM Studios. The great thing about Walt Disney World is that there really is something for everyone, at each theme park. If you don't feel like doing one thing, right next door is something you're dying to do. This whole week had been more fun after more excitement after more fun after more awesome stuff.

And our last day was the best. I was sad, because it was our last day, and the week had been so incredible. But I was also so totally blissed out because it was my birthday, and my friends and our parents were really making it the most special day ever.

Anyway, after we had seen just about everything at Disney-MGM Studios (which is worth a whole scrapbook by itself), we went home, swam one last time, then put on dresses to go to dinner. We had each bought matching dresses at a fabulous shop at Downtown Disney. (It had taken us about two hours to find one that we all liked. We have pretty different tastes in clothes.) But we had finally settled on a cool cotton sundress, with short sleeves, pockets, and a dropped waist. It was covered with big, floppy flowers in bright colors. Jasmine and I both got yellow dresses with orange flowers. Ella and Yukiko both got pink dresses with hot pink flowers. And Ariel and Paula got matching blue dresses with green flowers. I loved having matching dresses. It was like we were showing everyone how connected we were.

For my birthday dinner we went to the fancy restaurant in Italy at the World Showcase in Epcot. It was *fantastico*! My parents had arranged for an actual birthday cake, and when the waiter brought it out, everyone in the whole restaurant sang "Happy Birthday." I felt pretty princessy.

Then it was back to the Magic Kingdom to watch the

night parade and fireworks one last time. As we got in line along the parade route, I noticed my friends exchanging winks and glances. What were they up to? I was so busy watching the preparade show that I couldn't worry about it. It was dark now, and lights had come on all over the Magic Kingdom. It was a perfect temperature outside, and the soft breeze made me feel as if the wind was giving me a gentle hug.

By the time the light parade had started, the crowd of people was about six deep. Fortunately, we were right in front and had a great view. I had never seen a nighttime parade at Walt Disney World, and let me tell you, it was so awesome.

The first float rolled by, playing one of my favorite Disney songs, and Jasmine turned to me with a smile.

"The DGs have a birthday present for you, too," she said, trying to make herself heard over the music.

"Huh?" I asked. "Just your being here is my present."

Jasmine shook her head. "Nope. You'll see."

The next float rolled slowly toward us. Mickey Mouse stood in the front, singing and dancing. I grabbed my mom's sleeve and pointed. She nodded, laughing. The float drifted to a halt right in front of our group. People crowded around and I felt myself getting separated from my parents. I tried to push my way back, but Jasmine grabbed my hand.

"Come on!" she yelled over the noise of the crowd. Unbelievably, she pulled me toward the float. Ariel, in back of me, grabbed my other hand. The other DGs were linked to her, so we made a chain snaking through the crowd.

"What are you doing?" I yelled to Jasmine, but she just smiled and pulled me toward the float. I felt like I was moving in a dream—you know those dreams where you think you're walking, but you don't actually feel your legs moving? That's what it was like. My eyes about bugged out of my head when the back of the float *opened up.* Jasmine tugged me into a dark doorway. There were three tiny steps, and I tripped on them. Behind me, Ariel and the others pushed their way in. Then the door closed behind Yukiko, and a light went on.

"What the heck is going on?" I cried.

"We're inside the float," Jasmine explained, as if it was totally normal. (It was so *not.*)

"Wha—what?" I stammered. That's me: Miss Witty. Good thing I read so much, huh?

In the next three minutes, the six of us scrambled into incredibly gorgeous costumes—and each one was designed for the right princess. Mine was the wonderful yellow ballgown I wore in the last scene of my movie. Ella had the silvery, shimmery gown from her fairy god-mother. Paula had an amazing tan dress, sewn all over with tiny beads and feathers. Jasmine had an adorable outfit with full, baggy pants, pointy-toed slippers, and a crop top, all in lavender. Ariel had a fabulous long dress that looked like seashells on top, and iridescent fish scales on the bottom. And Yukiko had a beautiful Snow White gown, the one she was wearing at the very end, when the prince kissed her and she came back to life.

We looked—awesome. More than awesome. We looked like *ourselves*.

"What is going on?" I asked again, in wonder.

"You'll see," said Jasmine. I felt the float start moving again, and grabbed a beam for support. Then a door in front of us opened. Through it I could see the dark night sky and some of the twinkling lights on the float. A big white hand reached down, and Jasmine led me forward. Mickey Mouse helped me up the steps to the very front of the float.

I swallowed hard as my five friends joined me on the float's platform. The crowd roared and clapped when they saw us. I just stared, terrified, not knowing what to do. I looked around and Jasmine was smiling and waving to the crowd. So were my friends. Like it was totally normal, something they did every day. "Paula, did you do the dishes?" "Oh, sorry, Mom. I was in the Disney parade just then."

As the float rolled forward, music started. It swelled louder and louder until it was all I could hear. It was my theme song. Well. That did it. I started singing along. I could really belt it out as loudly as I wanted, because no one could hear me over the recording.

As we drifted and swayed along the parade route, the crowd cheered. Lightbulbs were flashing everywhere. Overhead, the fireworks started, filling the sky with bursts and flowers of light and fire. Jasmine took one hand, and Yukiko took the other. I smiled at Jasmine wonderingly. She mouthed, "Happy Birthday."

And I started to cry.

Epilogue

I was crying with *happiness*, you guys. Duh! I don't even remember getting back to our Grand Vista home that night, but we must have, because I woke up on the floor of our bedroom the next morning.

"Hey!" I said groggily. "Wasn't I supposed to get the king-sized bed again?"

Ariel rolled over noisily. "Your birthday's over, princess," she mumbled. "Now go back to sleep."

Two days later, I rushed impatiently through the lunch

line in our school cafeteria. I ran to our usual table by the window and slid into my seat.

"Gol, it feels like twenty years have gone by since we sat here," I said, opening my lunchbag.

"Yeah. You're a regular Rip Van Isabelle," Paula said. She took a sip of her iced tea, and I made a face at her.

"You know what I mean," I said. "So many amazing things happened."

"Yeah, we do know what you mean," said Jasmine. "And look! Ta-da!" She pulled a pretty quilted scrapbook out of her backpack. "It's finished! And it's yours. Another birthday present."

"Oh, Jasmine," I whispered, opening the cover. "This is going to be all of ours, all the Disney Girls. We'll take turns keeping it."

Jasmine had transferred everyone's diary entries into the scrapbook, along with tons of photographs we had all taken. It was so great to see a picture of our house, and the swimming pool, and a thousand other pictures of all of us doing amazing, funny, scary, and awesome things. For practically the whole lunch period we crowded around the scrapbook, reading what each other had written and laughing at the pictures. We were all so homesick for the Walt Disney World Resort that we were ready to go back that minute.

Right before the bell rang, I slapped my hand to my forehead.

"I almost forgot! My mom handed me a pack of photos this morning that she had just gotten back. It's the last roll. It should have us in the parade."

I ripped open the package and started to fan out the photos. Sure enough, my mom's good camera had actually managed to get some pretty great shots of the parade, even though it had been at night.

As we started to pore over them, first my forehead wrinkled, then I noticed Jasmine frowning in confusion. We all looked up and met each other's eyes.

"This is weird," Paula said bluntly.

"I don't get it," said Ariel.

"You guys . . . " I said slowly, staring at the photos. "This was magic. Magic took us there. We trusted magic to take us where it wanted us to go. This is what it did. It's showing us that we passed the test, whatever it was."

Silently we looked at the pictures one by one. The noise and clanking of kids eating lunch faded as we lost ourselves in the images. You see, my mom's pictures had captured reality. In every one of those photographs, you could see the six of us on the float. And in every picture, we were ourselves, our real selves, the selves we are inside. We looked like princesses, six of them, all different, yet all with a magical glow around us.

"What's your mom going to say when she sees these?" Ella asked in a hushed tone.

I shook my head. "I don't know. I don't even know if she'll see them the way we see them. She's not into, you know . . ."

"Magic," said Yukiko.

I nodded, then slowly gathered the photos and slipped them back into their envelope. "I'll come over this afternoon and we can put them into the scrapbook," I told Jasmine, and she nodded.

Then I took a deep breath. We all slid back into our seats. I felt as if I had just seen a total eclipse of the sun or something.

Across the table, Paula smiled at me.

"We're awesome," she said.

"We're fabulous," Ariel agreed.

"We're Disney Girls," I said. And suddenly, we were laughing, because that said it all.

In nine years of knowing Kenny McIlhenny, I thought I had seen him at his worst. I was wrong. Until now, his absolute worst behavior had been child's play compared to what he was doing now.

It was bad enough, his parents being away, so Kenny had to stay at our house. (We even had to share a bathroom! Eww!) And the fact that he brought his huge, slobbery dog, Otto, with him did not help things any. I had started keeping my shoes on in the house, because Otto actually drooled on the floor sometimes. I won't even describe how that feels in bare feet. Plus, Kenny had chicken pox, and I had to help take care of him!

But the thing that was really getting my goat was how he acted all sugary-sweet in front of my parents. Then, when they were gone, he was majorly rotten to me. "Yo, Isabelle, more juice, huh?" he would say. "Hey, Izzy, can you fluff this pillow for me?" (I hate being called Izzy.) "Iz? That sun is right in my eyes. Fix the miniblinds, will ya?" "Iz? Don't you guys get ESPN? There's a drag race on today."

Somehow, he managed to time it so that if I told him to fluff his own dang pillow, my mom would overhear. Then I would get a lecture about being thoughtful to sick people.

I'm telling you, he pushed me too far. I mean, I guess there's no excuse for what I did. I'm just trying to explain how it happened. All I know is, it seemed totally worth it. It was the most brilliant idea I'd ever had. And it brought the Beast to his knees.

Read all the books in the
Disney Girls series!

#1 *One of Us*

Jasmine is thrilled to be a Disney Girl. It means she has four best friends—Ariel, Yukiko, Paula, and Ella. But she still doesn't have a *best* best friend. Then she meets Isabelle Beaumont, the new girl. Maybe Isabelle could be Jasmine's *best* best friend—but could she be a *Disney Girl*?

#2 *Attack of the Beast*

Isabelle's next-door neighbor Kenny has been a total Beast for as long as she can remember. But now he's gone too far: he secretly videotaped the Disney Girls singing and dancing and acting silly at Isabelle's slumber party. Isabelle vows to get the tape back, but how will she ever get past the Beast?

#3 *And Sleepy Makes Seven*

Mrs. Hayashi is expecting a baby soon, and Yukiko is praying that this time it'll be a girl. She's already got six younger brothers and stepbrothers, and this is her last chance for a sister. All of the Disney Girls are hoping that with a little magic, Yukiko's fondest wish will come true.

#4 *A Fish Out of Water*

Ariel in ballet class? That's like putting a fish in the middle of the desert! Even though Ariel's the star of her swim team, she decides that she wants to spend more time with the other Disney Girls. So she joins Jasmine and Yukiko's ballet class.

But has Ariel made a mistake, or will she trade in her flippers for toe shoes forever?

#5 *Cinderella's Castle*

The Disney Girls are so excited about the school's holiday party. Ella decides that the perfect thing for her to make is an elaborate gingerbread castle. But creating such a complicated confection isn't easy, even for someone as super-organized as Ella. And her stepfamily just doesn't seem to understand how important this is to her. Ella could really use a fairy godmother right now. . . .

#6 *One Pet Too Many*

Paula's always loved animals, any animal. Who else would have a pet raccoon, not to mention three cats, three dogs, four finches, and fish? When Paula finds a lost armadillo, though, her parents say, "No more pets!"—and that's that. But how much trouble could an armadillo be? Plenty, as Paula discovers—especially when she's trying to keep it a secret from her parents.

#7 *Adventure at Walt Disney World:*
A Disney Girls Super Special

The Disney Girls are so excited. The three pairs of *best* best friends are going to spend a week together at Walt Disney World. Find out how the Disney Girls' magical wishes come true as they have the adventure of their lives.

continued . . .

#8 *A Beastly Visitor*

Isabelle is thrilled when she finds out that her beastly neighbor, Kenny, will be going away on vacation for a week with his family. Then Kenny comes down with chicken pox—and he has to stay at Isabelle's house for the week! She might be tempted to feel bad for Kenny—if he wasn't being his usual beastly self. With the help of the Disney Girls and a little magic, she decides to give Kenny a taste of *her* own medicine.

#9 *Good-bye, Jasmine?*

Jasmine has always been a little bit different from the other Disney Girls. She lives in the wealthy Wildwood Estates instead of in Willow Hill like her friends. But at least the girls get to see each other every day at Orlando Elementary. Then one day Jasmine's mother decides that it's time for her daughter to attend her alma mater, St John's boarding school. The Disney Girls are in shock. Will they have to say good-bye to one of their best friends?